King Thrushbeard

ALSO BY KURT WERTH

The Valiant Tailor
The Monkey, the Lion, and the Snake

Retold and Illustrated by

KURT WERTH

King Thrushbeard

THE VIKING PRESS   NEW YORK

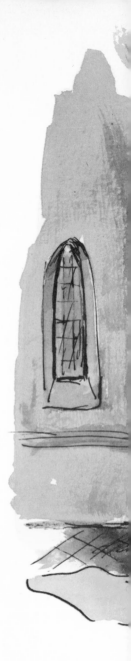

King Carol's daughter was very beautiful. She had golden hair and sparkling green eyes, and she was as tall and slender as a white birch tree. But lovely as she was, she had no kind word for anyone. King Carol's daughter was rude and arrogant.

None of her admirers pleased her. She found them all
ridiculous and dismissed them one after another with
words as sharp as thistles. After being patient for a long
time, the king made up his mind to put an end to her
ill-tempered ways. Somewhere there must be a young
man masterful enough to soften her prickliness!

He invited all the marriageable young noblemen from
miles around to come to a big banquet. They arrived at

the castle dressed in their finest clothes, riding horses
with trappings fashioned by the best silversmiths in the
land. The king himself went to welcome them at the gate,
then sent for his daughter to come to make her choice.
In the banqueting hall the master of the court lined the
nobles up in rows according to their ranks—first the
kings, then the princes, the dukes, the counts, and last
the barons. They stood looking expectantly toward the
door where the princess was to enter.

King Carol's daughter took her time and when at last she appeared, she was as elegant and disdainful as ever. She walked slowly along the rows of noblemen, and her manner of inspecting them was insulting. Fast and biting came her words.

One was too fat. "That wine barrel?" she asked.

Another was too tall. "That beanstalk?"

The third was too short. "From head to foot too brief, my dear."

The fourth was too sallow. "Pale as death," she said.

The next was too ruddy. "Just like a pomegranate!"

In this way she criticized every single one of them. A young king standing in the first row seemed particularly amusing to her. He was slim and tall, a pleasing, friendly-looking man altogether. But the naughty princess laughed in his face. "Your beard looks like a thrush's beak! I shall call you King Thrushbeard!"

It was not long before the noble company began taking their departure, first in ones and twos, then in threes and fours, soon in troops. The king was mortified and ashamed for his daughter.

"I vow," he shouted furiously, "that I shall marry you off to the first vagabond who comes to my door!"

The princess just laughed. She was a little frightened by his anger, but she did not believe he would ever do such a thing.

A few days later a wandering minstrel appeared in the palace courtyard and began to sing a fine ballad, accompanying himself on his lute.

Everybody stopped work to listen, enchanted by the strong, sweet voice. The king sent for the minstrel to come upstairs and asked him to sing again. The vagabond was all in rags and tatters. His hair and beard were so unkempt it was hard to tell where one began and the other left off. But his voice and tune-swept lute produced a master melody.

The king was well pleased and sent for his daughter. "I like your music," he said to the minstrel. "I like it so much that I am going to give you my daughter for a wife."

The man was speechless. But the daughter had plenty to say. She was horrified. The king stood firm. "I vowed to marry you off to the first vagabond who came to the door, and here he is."

In answer to the king's summons, the people of the court assembled, and the princess was married to the minstrel without delay.

She could not very well take to the road in her court dress, and a kitchen-maid's clothes were brought for her.

"Now," said the king, "for better or for worse you must
follow your husband. You have much to learn. Better be
on your way."

The princess began to sob, but the minstrel took her
arm, not unkindly, and led her out of the castle.

They started along the road in the spring sunshine. The air was warm, and white clouds moved in the blue sky. The whole world smelled of flowers.

The vagabond was happy and he whistled and sang. But whenever the princess wanted to rest he urged her on.

"The short can walk this far, also the lean and the fat. How is it that you, a princess, should tire? Is it the weight of your long golden hair, perhaps, or your green eyes heavy with anger?"

On, on, on they went, until they came to a large forest. He nodded to her and she sat down, exhausted, on a grassy bank. All around were blossoming bushes. The trees were splendid.

"Who owns this beautiful forest?" she asked the minstrel.

"It belongs to a handsome bearded king. It will go to his bride with her wedding ring."

The princess was puzzled, and said: "Oh, dearie me! This seems so weird—I wish I had married King Thrushbeard."

Soon he urged her to be up and away. They walked on until they came to pleasant, rolling meadowland. Larks rose into the sky, jubilantly pouring out their songs, and the princess was touched.

"Who owns this good land?" she asked.

"It belongs to a handsome bearded king. It will go to his bride with her wedding ring."

She sighed.

"Oh, dearie me! This seems so weird—I wish I had married King Thrushbeard."

They trudged until it seemed to the weary princess
that they had reached the ends of the earth. They came
to a big city, with ramparts that encircled the little gabled
houses and a splendid castle. People strolled in the shade
of plane trees along the narrow streets, and everyone looked
happy.

Again she wondered, Who owns this big city?

"It belongs to a handsome bearded king. It will go to
his bride with her wedding ring."

The princess put her face in her hands. "Oh, dearie
me! This seems so weird—I *wish* I had married King
Thrushbeard!"

Soon they left the city and walked along the road again. He helped her now, and she clung to his arm. At sunset, they arrived at a little tumbledown cabin, perched on a cliff by the riverbank. She asked, "Who owns this little cabin?"

He answered: "This is our house, where we shall live together."

She was so tired that she was thankful to have arrived even at such a humble place.

But she asked, "Where are the servants?"

"There are none. You have to use your own hands; they are the best servants." He pushed open the door. "Go in and make a fire while I fetch water from the well. You must prepare our meal. I am very hungry."

She had no idea how to kindle a fire, much less did she know how to cook. Helplessly she stared at him. The minstrel had to show her how to do everything. But he was patient with her and she learned quickly.

"At least your wits are sharp," he remarked.

Half asleep, they ate their frugal meal.

Early the next morning he woke her. "Get busy and clean the house!" he commanded. "You must know we have to earn our living. My ballad-singing alone is not enough. I shall show you how to weave baskets and then you must sell them."

He cut twigs from the willows near the river and brought them to the house. The princess tried hard to learn how to weave baskets, but the willow wood pinched her soft hands until she moaned with pain.

"Leave it!" he cried. "I see that your hands are much too soft for this. Better sit down and spin."

Obediently, she sat at the spinning wheel but the thread came now bunched, now thin. The poorest spinster in the country was more likely to sell her work. The princess was crimson with shame to be so useless.

"We are going to have a difficult time with you," grumbled the minstrel. "Let me think of something else."

Outside the cabin he strode up and down, considering. "I have it! I will get crockery from the old potter in the village and you will sell it in the market place. It is not difficult."

The princess's heart sank. "If people of my father's kingdom come and see me selling jugs and mugs, there will be no end to their mockery," she whispered to herself. But she had no choice. They did not want to die of hunger.

In the market square she spread out her stock of earthen utensils, and selling went better than she had expected. The folk there were kind and helpful, and the townspeople came and bought her wares and paid the price she asked. Everyone was polite to her. Blissfully she counted her earnings at the end of the day.

But the next morning she was sitting at a corner of the market place, surrounded by her brittle merchandise, when a drunken hussar came galloping into the square. His horse's feet came crashing down, and broke the pottery into a thousand pieces. Bursting into tears, the princess ran all the way home and told the minstrel what had happened.

"Why did you sit at the corner of the market place instead of in the middle?" he scolded. "This might never have happened!" But his hand was gentle on her hair. "Stop crying. It does not help. Go sit on the riverbank until your eyes are dry."

When she came back he told her, "They need a scullery maid in the castle. If you do good work you will be given your meals free."

So the king's daughter became a scullery maid. As the cook's helper, she had to peel the vegetables, wash the dishes, scrub the kitchen floor, and soon her hands were roughened and red. The cook was kind, however. "You poor, ignorant girl!" he said. "I shall need to teach you everything!"

And he showed her how to do her work well. He was a friendly man, and every evening saved tasty leftovers for her. She put them in little pots and took them home for the minstrel's supper.

One day the city rang with fanfares of trumpets. The young king was going to take a wife! News of the wedding spread swiftly through the streets. The people loved their king, and the crowds cheered lustily as they pelted off to observe the splendor of the arriving guests.

The castle was bustling with activity. In the royal kitchen the cook was beside himself—there was so much to be done! Cakes had to be baked and decorated, fat geese and pigs roasted, puddings and candied fruits prepared. . . . So many vegetables had to be cleaned and peeled that the scullery maid was almost in despair.

"How can you whistle and sing so cheerfully when you're so overworked?" she asked the other servants.

"Because this is a happy day!" the pastry cook replied. "We rejoice that our young king is to be married at last."

"And may his bride be as kind and virtuous as he!" said an old serving-woman.

The princess pondered this, and said: "Oh, dearie me! This is so weird—I wish I had married King Thrushbeard!"

She wanted to finish her work and go home, but today, especially, she must wait for the leftovers.

When she heard the sound of gay music and the din of voices from the ballroom, she could not resist the temptation to run up and peek. Through a half-open door she saw the dazzling lights of hundreds of candles. She saw the ladies and gentlemen dressed in silks and velvets. And here she was, a king's daughter, turned into a kitchen maid and banished from all the beauty and gaiety! Why?

Tears came to her eyes. She thought of the good things she would have to take home to the minstrel after the wedding feast, and knew she would have them only through the kindness of the people in the kitchen. Kindness! When had she ever been kind? When had she, a king's daughter, been as thoughtful as the king's servants?

Her lovely head was bent low and her green eyes swam with tears as she turned away from the gay scene in the ballroom—and ran straight into King Thrushbeard! The young king was dressed in richly embroidered garments, and wore a gold chain around his neck. His face lighted up with a warm smile and he said: "Do you not know me? Come, a dance."

Scarlet with confusion, she shrank back, but he drew her, protesting, into the ballroom. The wedding guests laughed, and the mortified scullery maid wanted to sink a thousand fathoms under the earth.

King Thrushbeard held her still. "Don't mind them and don't run away, my beautiful. I have a story to tell you. You should know that I was the ragged minstrel who took you to the cabin. I was the drunken hussar who broke your earthenware. You had many lessons to learn, but you have done well. The masquerade is over now. I have loved you always. Come, let's celebrate our wedding!"

The ladies-in-waiting led her away and arrayed her in a golden gown embroidered with pearls. In such a gown and with her golden hair she was as radiant as Venus in the evening sky.

Her father, King Carol, was overjoyed that she had so good a husband as King Thrushbeard. The heralds blew a flourish on their trumpets, the pipers played their merriest music, and such festivities began as had never been known in the kingdom before.

So the scullery maid who was a naughty princess became the good wife of King Thrushbeard. They lived
together like two birds in a nest—which is not always
peaceable, of course. And whenever the princess began
to show signs of ill temper the king had only to stroke
his beard.